Amazon Adventure

Penn Mullin

High Noon Books
No

Cover Design and Interior Illustrations: Damon Rarey

International Standard Book Number: 0-57128-009-X

10 09 08 07 06 05 04 03 02
0 9 8 7 6 5 4 3

You'll enjoy all the High Noon Books. Write for
a free full list of titles.

Contents

Lots of stories appeared in the newspapers after the four seventh graders in Miss Lake's class came home from their special trip to Europe. They had been given the trip by a mysterious "Mrs. X," who arranged a mystery for them in each place they visited. Marco Santos, a pilot, read about the kids and decided he wanted to show them *his* country – Brazil – and other South American countries – during their summer vacation. And he would fly them everywhere himself – in his own plane!

CHAPTER 1

The River Sea

"That can't be a *river*!" Juan said. "It's got to be the ocean." He pointed out the window of the small plane.

"No, that's the Amazon River down there," Marco, the pilot of the plane, told him. "*O Rio Mar*" – the River Sea. That's what we call it in South America. In some places it is 200 miles wide where it meets the Atlantic Ocean."

"A 200-mile-wide river! And we're going on it in a little boat?" Lisa asked.

"That can't be a river," Juan said.
"It's got to be the ocean."

"Don't worry," laughed Marco. "The river gets smaller as we go up it. Mostly you will be able to see both banks of it from the boat."

"I don't know," Lisa said. "This boat ride along the Amazon sounds creepy. Snakes and alligators and jungle all around us."

"Look," said Miss Lake, their teacher. "You can see the Amazon's muddy water pushing way out into the ocean."

"It dumps a half-*trillion* gallons a day into the Atlantic!" Marco said. "Enough for all the houses in your country for five months!"

"Wow! That's amazing. How deep is the river?" Amy asked Marco.

"In places, 200 feet," he said. "Deep

enough for ocean ships to travel 2,300 miles up it to Peru on the Pacific Coast!"

"Is the Amazon the longest river in the world?" Justin asked.

"No, the Nile River in Egypt is longer. But the Amazon is 4,000 miles long," Marco told him.

"Look! What's that huge wave down there?" cried Juan. He pointed out of the plane window to the river below.

"Oh, that's the *pororoca* (pour-ah-ROE-kah)! 'The big roar' they call it. We are lucky to get to see it. Once a month that tide rolls up the river from the Atlantic Ocean," Marco said. "It makes a wave fifteen feet high!"

"What happens if you're in its way?" Lisa

asked.

Marco said, "I guess it's too bad for you. The pororoca destroys everything in its path. But you can hear it coming."

"I'm glad we're not down on the river yet," Amy said. "How awful to hear that big roar coming at you!"

"You'll hear other roars, too," laughed Juan. "Jaguars in the jungle."

"Yes, but they like to stay hidden. Unless they get hungry," Marco chuckled.

"I hope we see one," Justin said. "I can't wait to get down on the river."

"*I* can!" Lisa said. "The Amazon looks a lot safer from up here at 10,000 feet!"

CHAPTER 2

Secrets of the Amazon

"I'm ready to get to Manaus (ma-NAH-us) and get on our boat," said Justin. "This is one long plane ride!"

"We're almost there," Marco told his passengers. "And you're right, Justin. It *is* a long way. We have followed the Amazon almost 900 miles. The city of Manaus is exactly halfway up the Amazon."

"We flew it in just a few hours today. Just think if you were in a little canoe. That's the way the first explorers came down the Amazon," said Miss Lake. "It took them eight months!"

"Months of floods, fevers, blizzards, no food. It's amazing that they ever made it," Marco said.

"Blizzards?" said Amy. "In South America?"

"Remember, the Andes Mountains are very high. That's where the Spanish explorers started from in 1541," Miss Lake said. "They were looking for the 'cities of gold' they had heard about."

"Did they ever find them?" Lisa asked.

"No, they never did," Marcos answered.

"That's a neat mystery," Juan said. "So the

'cities of gold' might still be there."

"No one knows. The Amazon is very large. It has many mysteries. Look at how the trees seem to go on forever." Marco pointed down.

"They look like miles of broccoli from up here," Justin said.

"You would think about food!" Lisa laughed.

"Well, it is getting near dinner time, isn't it?" Justin said.

"We'll eat aboard the Eva tonight," Marco told them. "My friend José is fixing a special Brazilian dinner for you."

"You take such good care of us, Marco! We are seeing South America in style!" Miss Lake told him.

"It is easy in my plane. And I want to show you everything. I am proud of my country," said Marco. "When I read about your travels in Europe I got an idea. 'I'm going to bring them to see *my* country,' I said to myself. And here you are!"

"And are we ever lucky!" Juan said.

"Look! There's the city of Manaus," Marco told the group. "Near where those two rivers join."

"That one river is totally black!" said Lisa. "It looks like a river of oil."

"That's the *Rio Negro,* the Black River. It gets its color from swamps up in Colombia and

Venezuela where it begins," Marco said. "O.K. Time to start down to Manaus!"

The airport looked very tiny and far away. Marco slowly turned the plane so that it was lined up perfectly with the runway. The radio crackled on and a voice said in Portuguese, "94 T cleared to land!"

"Why do they speak Portuguese here in Brazil?"Amy asked Marco. She was sitting in the co-pilot's seat beside him.

"Because Spain and Portugal ruled most of South America until the early 1800's," Marco answered. Then he pulled back on the handles at his side and the engines slowed.

"Will you push that button a little please?"

Marco asked Amy. "That will put down the flaps on our wings."

They could feel the plane slowing more. The land grew closer. Marco pulled back further on his wheel. The one in front of Amy moved back, too.

"It's almost in my lap!" Amy laughed.

"My turn to sit there next trip," Juan said. "Remember that!"

Now their plane seemed to be just hanging in the air. Then they heard the wheels screech as they touched the runway. They were down! "Welcome to Manaus!" Marco announced.

CHAPTER 3

Off to the *Eva*!

"José, please drive us through the center of Manaus. I want to show off this city," Marco said. They were all riding in José's big van.

"It is my pleasure. Manaus is still beautiful. But so crowded. One million people now. And not enough jobs. There it is – the *Teatro Amazonas* (tay-AH-tro am-a-ZO-nas) – our opera house. Doesn't it look like Paris?" José pointed across the plaza.

"This was built back in the 1890's" Marco

told the kids and their teacher. "Can you believe Manaus was one of the richest cities in the world then?"

"Why was it so rich?" Amy asked.

"Rubber. Thousands of trees nearby were 'tapped.' A cut was made in their bark. Latex dripped out. This is what rubber is made from," Marco said. "In the year 1890, all the world's rubber came from right here."

"People had lots of money to spend. So they made Manaus look like a city in Europe," José said. "But then it all ended. Poof!"

"Why?" Juan asked.

"Someone discovered that rubber trees would grow very well in China," Marco said.

"And it was much cheaper to make rubber there. So Manaus was no longer a boom town."

"But we have places like this to remind us of those days," said José. "So now I'll take you down to my boat, Eva. I hope you will like her."

"José is a wonderful riverboat pilot," Marco said. "You'll be very safe with him."

"I don't let many *caimans* (cay-MAHNS) get on board, do I, Marco?" José laughed.

"Caimans? What are they?" Lisa asked.

"Black alligators. Don't worry. José usually runs his boat too fast for them to climb on board," laughed Marco.

"I'm not sure I want to get on this boat," Lisa said. "Is it high off the water?"

"Oh, yes, don't worry," José told her. "Look. We're coming to the docks now. Manaus is very famous for its floating market. The stores are on boats and floating docks. They sell the freshest fish in the world, the best fruits."

"Why are the docks floating?" Justin wanted to know.

"Because the tide here rises fifty feet in the rainy season," Marco said. "And that's why so many houses are built on stilts."

"Here's my Eva," José said. "All ready for you to come aboard." He parked the van beside a forty-foot white riverboat tied up at the dock. They all got out and José led them aboard.

"This is really neat," Justin said as the kids

"Here's my Eva," José said.

walked around the boat. "I like the way it's a double decker. Up here is where I want to ride."

"So the snakes and caimans can't get you, right?" Amy laughed.

"Ha ha. I bet you freak out the first snake we see in the water!" said Justin.

"Snakes aren't in the water," Lisa told him.

"What? You don't know about the *anacondas*?" Juan stared at her. "They live in the river and can swallow an animal as big as a calf!"

"I'm going to check this out with José," Lisa said. "I bet you're making this up!"

Suddenly they heard a bell ringing down in the Eva's galley. "Dinner!" José called out.

"Hooray! I'm starved," Justin said.

"Better not let him get to dinner first," Juan said. "There won't be anything left for us!"

There was one long table in the small dining room. It was piled high with plates of fish and vegetables. José stood beside the table, all smiles.

"Welcome to the Eva!" he said.

"How did you do all this, José? We just came aboard a half hour ago!" said Marco.

"I have my good helper, Elcio. He makes magic with our river fish," José told them. Elcio came in from the galley and waved to everyone. His face lit up with a wide smile.

"I made my special *feigao* (FAY-joe) and

arroz (ah-ROZ) for you tonight. Come, sit down and enjoy," Elcio told them all.

Justin said, "This rice and bean dish is super. And what kind of fish is this? I love it." He helped himself to another piece.

"Shark. Caught this morning," Elcio told him. "Very near here."

"Oh, yes. Many saltwater fish swim this far up the Amazon," Marco said.

"This river has *everything* in it! No way am I swimming on this trip! And I have that new bikini, too." Amy made a sad face.

Suddenly they saw a tall thin man coming into the dining room. He was carrying a pile of notebooks and did not smile at anyone.

"Mr. Bates! Welcome! Come join us," José called out. "I'm glad you found my boat."

"It wasn't easy. All the boats look alike in this harbor," Mr. Bates said. "I've had a long hard trip down here. Please just tell me where my cabin is."

"Surely. Follow me," José said. He left the dining room, and Mr. Bates followed him.

"I forgot to tell you that José has an extra passenger on this trip," Marco said. "Mr. Bates is a scientist who wants to go up the Amazon. But he won't tell José why. He is searching for something."

"Sounds spooky," Amy said slowly. "I wonder what Mr. Bates is after."

CHAPTER 4

A Mystery in the Jungle

"We're ready to go! Justin, Lisa, you can untie those ropes," José yelled. He started the engines and the Eva slowly backed away from the dock.

The kids stood on the deck with Marco and Miss Lake. They looked out at the busy harbor of Manaus all around them. Canoes and small fishing boats were everywhere. People in them shouted out, "Peixe! (PAY-she) (fish) Bananas! Guarana (GUAH-rah-na) (fruit)!"

"Look, you can see how the houses are

built way up on stilts." Marco showed the kids. "This harbor floods each rainy season."

"When is that?" Lisa asked.

"November to June," Marco said. "We are here at the best time – the start of July."

"And it is *hot*! My shirt is soaking wet already," Juan said. "I may have to forget the anacondas and dive into the river later."

"Good thing we had those mosquito nets over our bunks last night," said Amy. "We would have been eaten alive."

"Think of those poor explorers in the 1500's," Miss Lake said. "The mosquitoes nearly drove them insane."

"And me in the 1990's – they may drive me

insane!" Justin laughed as he swatted at one.

"Where is the scientist this morning?" Lisa asked. "Has anyone seen him?"

"I really want to know what he's looking for," Juan said. "Why is it a big secret?"

"Maybe he's looking for those lost cities of gold," Amy laughed.

"Well, we'll be on the river with him for about five days," Miss Lake said. "Maybe we'll get a clue before we leave the boat. Oh, I almost forgot – did you all mail your postcards home from Manaus?"

"Yes," Lisa laughed. "But I hope this isn't my last postcard home. The Amazon sounds scary to me."

"Don't worry! This is going to be a great adventure!" Miss Lake said.

The Eva moved slowly up the Amazon, away from the crowded docks. Soon the dark jungle came right up to the river's banks. Small shacks were tucked among the trees.

"The jungle takes over fast, doesn't it?" Marco said. "Makes you feel pretty small. Watch the trees – you might see monkeys now, or the bright-colored macaw parrots."

"Or a boa constrictor hanging down," Juan chuckled wickedly.

José waved at them from up on the Eva's top deck. His steering wheel was there. And he had a good view of the river ahead.

Suddenly Mr. Bates came up on deck. He nodded at everyone. Then he took out his binoculars. He began to stare into the trees.

"He's looking for something, that's for sure," Justin said. "I wish we knew what."

"What's that in the water?" cried Amy.

Marco laughed. "That's a *manatee*! It looks like a seal. They're very friendly. Manatees feed on underwater grasses and have fun just being lazy."

"Doesn't sound like a bad life," Juan laughed. "Just laze on down the Amazon."

"How did this river get named the Amazon?" Lisa asked Marco.

"The Spanish explorers gave it that name in

Marco laughed. "That's a manatee!"

the 1500's. They reported seeing giant women warriors on the shore," Marco said. "These warriors reminded them of women in a Greek myth who were called Amazons."

"Maybe that's what our scientist is looking for – the lost giant women of the Amazon," laughed Justin.

"The jungle is so thick and dark. *Anything* could be hiding in there," said Lisa.

"Yes, the rain forest is all around you now. It's the largest rain forest in the world," Marco told them. "It began 140 million years ago as an inland sea in the age of dinosaurs."

"And it is in great danger," Miss Lake said. "Farmers and ranchers burn and cut more trees each year. When rain forests began, they covered about 6 million square miles on earth. Now they cover only 3 million."

"That's pretty scary," Juan whistled.

"Think of the State of Florida. An area that big is ripped from the rain forest each year," said Marco. "Gone forever."

"What if things keep on this way?" Amy asked.

"The rain forests could just totally disappear," said Miss Lake.

"Aren't people trying to save them?" asked Justin.

"Yes, a group of countries made a plan to help protect the rain forest here. But they need to get timber, coffee, and rubber out of the forest, too. This brings a lot of money to these poor countries," said Marco.

"Wouldn't it be awful to have the rain forest just disappear?" Lisa said.

"Thousands of plants, animals, and insects would disappear, too," Miss Lake said.

"Almost half of earth's oxygen supply is renewed in the rain forests," Marco added. "It is formed by the huge number of plants growing there. You won't believe how *thick* that forest is when you go in it!"

Suddenly there was a shout from behind them. It was Mr. Bates! He was jumping up and down and shouting, "Stop! Stop the boat!"

CHAPTER 5

Into the Rain Forest!

José slowly steered the Eva over to the river bank. Mr. Bates was running up and down the deck. He kept looking into the jungle with his binoculars.

"What's wrong? What do you see?" José called down to the scientist.

"The giant sloth! I saw him. I know I did. He was watching us. In the jungle. I have to go after him. Wait for me here!" And Mr. Bates hurried off the boat.

Everyone else just stood on the deck watching him go into the jungle.

"So – that's what he's after. The giant sloth," José said. "No wonder he kept it a secret in Manaus. A lot of scientists are looking for the sloth. There seems to be a race to see who will be the one to catch it!"

"*What* is a giant sloth?" Amy asked.

"Well, the jungle Indians talk of a creature with a giant bear's body and a monkey's face," José told her. "It stands tall like a man and makes a terrible roar."

"Sounds like our Bigfoot in America," Juan said. "People have seen his tracks, but no one has ever caught him."

"Scientists now think this creature is the giant sloth. This kind of animal should have died 8,000 years ago," José said.

"But it's roaming this jungle right here! Talk about creepy!" Lisa said.

"Did Mr. Bates take a rope or net with him, José?" Miss Lake asked.

"He left so fast I couldn't tell," said José. "I guess we just wait here and see."

"And listen for screams," said Justin.

"Will you stop?" Lisa yelled at him.

"Well, we don't have to stay on board. How about a walk in the rain forest?" Marco asked.

"But what about the giant sloth?" Amy asked. "He could be anywhere in there."

"I bet he is far away by now with Mr. Bates chasing him," laughed José. "You all go for a walk and I'll watch the boat."

"We won't go far," Marco said. "Ring the bell if you want us, José."

Everyone put on lots of mosquito repellent and filled up their water bottles. Then they followed Marco into the forest.

Soon they were deep into a world of dark green. The air was hot and damp around them.

"Just stop for a moment now and listen." The group did as Marco said. "Can you hear the call of the parrots high in the trees? Listen to the soft rustlings all around you. The forest is alive.

"It's beautiful," whispered Amy. "I feel like I'm in another world. Like inside one of those glass terrariums. Green and warm."

"Look at the size of these flowers!" Miss Lake pointed to a huge yellow orchid growing out of a low tree branch.

"The rain forest grows giant *everything*!" Marco laughed. "Bamboo can grow as tall as a five-story building!"

"Why is it so dark in here?" Juan asked.

"Look high above you. See how tight together the trees are? They form a *canopy* that keeps out most light," Marco said. "There is a whole world up there in the treetops. Eagles, monkeys, parrots. Down here is its own world, too. Just one tree has more than 1,700 kinds of ants and beetles in it!"

"How much rain does this forest get?" Miss Lake asked.

"About a hundred and fifty inches a year," Marco said. "It stays wet down here all the time. The soil is full of decay."

Suddenly Lisa screamed.

"What is it?" cried Miss Lake.

Lisa couldn't speak. She just pointed at the tree in front of her. Then everybody saw it. A huge green snake was stretched out along the tree trunk. Its color matched the tree's color exactly.

"I almost put my hand on it!" Lisa said.

"An emerald tree boa!" Marco told them. "Lisa, you have sharp eyes! Look how well his color protects him. There he goes. He's off to find a fat bird for lunch."

"Did I hear *lunch*?" Justin asked.

"We'll head back soon. I've been listening for José's bell. I wonder if Mr. Bates has had any luck!" said Marco.

"Maybe the giant sloth will run this way! Then we'll get to be famous!" Amy said.

"Hey, what's that noise? Listen! Do you hear that crunching sound?" Juan asked.

"Uh oh," said Marco. "Army ants. Coming our way. Good time to head back to the boat. We don't want to get in their way!"

"Army ants! I've read about them!" Justin said. "They eat *everything* in their path. They pick your bones clean!"

"How could ants do that?" Juan asked. "There would have to be a lot of them."

"There are!" Marco said. "They march in rows six inches wide and more than a mile long. They can move six feet a minute, too!"

"I'm out of here!" Justin said. "I'd rather not be an ant's lunch!"

"He'd have a great treat," Lisa laughed.

"You'll pay for that," Justin warned.

Suddenly they heard the Eva's bell.

"José must want us back there quickly. He is ringing the bell hard. Follow me!" Marco led them back towards the boat. Behind them the crunching sound grew closer.

Soon they could see the Eva at the river's edge. José and Mr. Bates were standing on the deck talking loudly.

"It is too dangerous," José was saying. "There are too many dead trees in the water there. We might hit one."

"But the sloth is in there. You have to take me. I know where he is now," the scientist argued. "I'll get him this time."

"But what about my passengers?" said José. "What if my boat sinks going after your sloth?"

CHAPTER 6

Man Overboard!

The Eva pulled slowly away from the shore. Then it turned into a smaller side part of the river. The jungle crowded in close to the banks, and the water was slow and dark.

"I must be crazy to do this," José told Marco. "The water is full of trees that can wreck us." He watched the river carefully as he steered the Eva. "But I will go only one mile. This is what I told Bates. If he doesn't find the sloth, we turn around."

Mr. Bates sat on the deck railing and stared into the trees. He had a net and a rope in his hand. The Eva was very close to the shore now. Miss Lake and the kids crowded along the railing and looked into the jungle.

"How close did you get to the sloth?" Juan asked the scientist.

"About twenty feet. I had my net all ready. But then he jumped into the river," Mr. Bates said. "He swam to those trees."

Suddenly there was a terrible roar. It came from the jungle beside them.

"It's the sloth!" cried Mr. Bates. "He's right in there. Pull the boat in, José!"

The Eva began to move in to the shore.

Suddenly there was a loud *thud*! The whole boat shook. They'd hit something. The boat jerked sideways. Then there was a splash.

"Mr. Bates!" yelled Justin. "He fell in!"

The scientist began thrashing wildly in the water. Marco raced down towards the deck.

"Caiman!" screamed José from up top. He pointed down into the river. The long black alligator was heading straight for Mr. Bates!

There was no time to think. Justin jumped in. He grabbed Mr. Bates by the shirt. But the man's arms came up and started to pull Justin under! Water filled Justin's nose and mouth. He felt himself going down.

Suddenly someone pushed him up! Air!

Someone tore the arms away from his neck. He heard screams. And then he saw Marco pulling Mr. Bates towards the boat. Everybody was yelling from the boat deck. Justin slowly swam towards it. Hands reached down and pulled him up. Mr. Bates lay on the deck. Marco was working over him, getting him breathing again.

"Justin! You're safe!" cried Miss Lake. "You were amazing – jumping in like that." She hugged him tightly. "I'm so proud of you."

"But Marco saved him," Justin said, shivering. José put a blanket around him.

"You kept Bates up above the water. Underwater, the caiman would have had him. Elcio hit the caiman with a club just before it got to you," José said.

Elcio stood by the rail, club in hand. He smiled at Justin. "I am good at other things besides cooking!" he laughed.

Mr. Bates was sitting up now. He was trying to talk. "Thank you," he said to Marco. "You saved my life."

"I had help. Justin kept you from going under right away. He's a brave boy," Marco said. "And Elcio drove off the caiman."

Justin went over to Marco. "You pulled me up. I thought for sure I was a goner." He shook hands with Marco. "Thank you," hc said.

Mr. Bates looked up at the group. "I'm a very lucky man. And a very selfish one," he said. "I risked your lives to go after that sloth. José, is your boat O.K.?

"Yes, we were lucky! No holes, no leaks. But we stay on the main river from now on," said José. "We start right after lunch!"

"Did I hear *lunch*?" Justin asked.

"Justin, now we *know* you're just fine." Lisa laughed. "José, you said the magic word – *lunch*! We've got our old Justin back. And we're sure glad!"